CHACHA CHAUDHARY AND BYE BYE KACHRA
BREATHING FRESH AIR.
EARLY MORNING EXERCISE KEEPS YOU FIT.
IT'S GREEN EVERYWHERE.
CHACHA JI! YOU TAKE A WALK WHILE I DO MY EXERCISE.
A THUNDERSTORM IS COMING.
NEED TO TAKE SHELTER.
I CAN'T FIND CHACHA JI.

PEOPLE START RUNNING TO SAVE THEMSELVES FROM THE STORM.
THE CITY IS GETTING DIRTY.
GARBAGE IS BEING SCATTERED ALL ACROSS THE CITY.
WE NEED TO CLEAN THIS UP.
FRESH AIR HAS TURNED FOUL DUE TO THE GARBAGE.
THE WHOLE CITY IS NOW STINKING.
SABU ! HUGE AMOUNTS OF GARBAGE HAVE BEEN SCATTERED DUE TO THE STORM.
HELP US TO GET IT CLEARED.
SURE !
IT'S SMELLING A LOT.
HUBBA ... HUBBAA !!

AFTER THUNDERSTORM STOPS.
HERE IT GOES. IT TAKES A LOT OF EFFORT TO CLEAN THE CITY.
IT'S A BIG LANDFILL.
WE NEED TO DO SOMETHING ABOUT IT.
ELSE IT'LL GROW BIGGER AND BIGGER.
HOW DO WE SOLVE SUCH A PROBLEM? LET'S THINK.
CHACHA CHAUDHARY CAN FIND A SOLUTION FOR IT. LET'S GO TO HIM.
CHACHA JI ! PLEASE FIND US A SOLUTION TO CLEAR THIS GARBAGE.
IT'S A GRAVE PROBLEM. IT'S VERY IMPORTANT TO SEGREGATE WASTE AT THE SOURCE.

AT THE SOURCE!!!
WASTE IN OUR HOUSE SHOULD BE SEPARATED IN TWO BINS. ONE FOR DRY AND OTHER FOR WET.
WE CAN MAKE COMPOST OUT OF OUR WET WASTE AND USE IT FOR OUR PLANTS AND PARKS.
MY FRIEND BHARAT WILL SHOW YOU HOW TO MAKE COMPOST.
COLLECT ALL YOUR WET WASTE IN THIS BIN.
ADD COCO DUST AND DRY LEAVES TIME TO TIME.

KEEP TURNING FROM TIME TO TIME AND IT WILL BE CONVERTED INTO COMPOST.
NOW YOU KNOW HOW TO MAKE COMPOST FROM WASTE.
40% TO 50% OF OUR WASTE CAN BE USED IN CREATING COMPOST.
PEOPLE START USING BLUE AND GREEN BIN.
NOW OUR CITY IS CLEAN.
CHACHA JI WITH ALL YOUR EFFORTS CITY HAS BECOME HEALTHY AND CLEAN.

WE CAN EARN CASH BY SELLING PLASTIC BOTTLES TO KABARIWALA.
... AND MAKE DECORATIVE ITEMS FROM THE WASTE.
PLASTIC CAN BE RECYCLED FOR MAKING ROADS, BRICKS, PIPES.
NOW YOU MUST PUT YOUR DRY WASTE INTO BLUE BIN.
LET'S MAKE A PLEDGE TO SEGREGATE OUR WASTE INTO BLUE AND GREEN BINS TO MAKE GANDHIJI'S DREAM OF SWACHH BHARAT MISSION A SUCCESS.
BYE BYE KACHRA WELCOME SWACHHATA
MY SWACHH BHARAT.

CHACHA CHAUDHARY SUPERSTAR

WILL YOU GIVE PERMISSION CHACHAJI ?
ON ONE CONDITION.
I'LL ONLY PLAY THE ROLE OF CHACHI IN THE FILM.
IT WILL BE AMAZING WHEN SUPERSTAR SAJANI DEVA WILL LIFT ME IN HIS ARMS.
YES, DEAR. YOU'LL SURELY ENJOY.
AFTER LIFTING YOU SAJANI DEVA WILL LAND UP IN HOSPITAL.
I'LL GIVE YOU A ROLE IN ANOTHER MOVIE.

I PERMIT YOU, MR. MURGAPPA.
THANKS !
WE ARRANGE FOR THE SHOOTING.
FILM SHOOTING.
ACTION !
FILM SHOOTING GOING ON. THE HERO IN CHACHAJI'S MAKE UP IS SURROUNDED BY CHACHAJI IS THE GOONS WATCHING THE SHOOTING.
THOD !!
SAJANI DEVA IS A GOOD ACTOR. ACTING JUST LIKE ME.

2 ACTUAL GOONS ARE STANDING AND WATCHING THE SHOOTING.
DAKARO, YOU ARE SEEING SUPER STAR SAJANI DEVA!
YES, HE'S BEATING MANY GOONS ALTOGETHER.
IT'S A FILM, ACTUALLY HE'S SUCH A BIG COWARD THAT EVEN IF HE SEES A MOUSE, HE AWAY TO FOREIGN IN HIS SPECIAL PLANE.
MEANS, IT WILL BE EASY TO KIDNAP HIM.
YOU'RE RIGHT.
WE'LL KIDNAP HIM TOMORROW.

NEXT DAY.
LIGHT!
CAMERA!!
CHACHA CHOUDHARY
PROD. NO.
SCENE
TAKE
ROLL
SOUND
DATE
Today
DIRECTOR
ACTION!
BANG!
THUD! THUD!!
TODAY WE'LL DO THE ACTION.
NO ONE SHOULD MOVE. WE'RE KIDNAPPING THE SUPERSTAR, SAJANI DEVA.

SAJANI DEVA, REMOVE THIS MAKE UP AND MOVE QUIETLY WITH US.
OK.
FIRST OF ALL I'LL REMOVE THE TURBAN.
SWISH !
SMASH !
HIT !
AAHHH !!
OUCH !!

YOU'RE GONE.
BANG !
NOTHING HAPPENED! ME.
SWISH !!

NOW SEE THE WONDER OF MY STICK.
SWISH !! SWOOSH !!
CHACHA CHAUDHARY ROTATES THE STICK IN A STYLE.
CHACHAJI THROWS THE STICK IN THE FRONT DIRECTION.
THUD !
AHHH !
THEN THE STICK TAKES A U-TURN AND COMES BACK.

DAKARO ! AH ! SUPER STAR SAJANI DEVA HAS THRASHED US BADLY.
IT IS SAID THAT HE'S AFRAID OF EVEN A MOUSE.
YOU'RE TALKING OF A MOUSE, LAST NIGHT HE WAS SO AFRAID OF A COCKROACH THAT HE ESCAPED IN HIS PLANE. WE COULDN'T DELAY OUR SHOOTING DUE TO HIM. SO…
… WE REQUESTED CHACHAJI TO ACT IN A FEW SCENES.
HE ACCEPTED OUR REQUEST.
AND YOU HAD TO DEAL WITH CHACHA CHAUDHARY HIMSELF.

AFTER SEEING YOUR ACTING AND ACTION, I'VE BECOME A GREAT FAN OF YOURS. I WANT TO TAKE YOU IN THE MOVIE INSTEAD OF SAJANI DEVA.
ARE YOU READY ?
NO, SORRY.
I'LL GO.
YOU SHOULD'VE SAID YES. AT LEAST I WOULD'VE BECOME YOUR HEROINE.
THAT'S WHY I REFUSED.
!!

CHACHA CHAUDHARY AND NATIONAL MUSEUM
HELLO, CHACHAJI. I'M MADAM KUSAAD.
I'M HER MANAGER GUTIYA.
WE'VE COME FROM NATIONAL MUSEUM.
MA'AM IS FOND OF MAKING STATUES OF INTER NATIONALLY FAMOUS PERSONALITIES AND DISPLAYING IN THE MUSEUM.
MA'AM WANTS TO MAKE YOUR STATUE ALSO.

DO AS YOU WISH.
THANKS CHACHAJI !
SOON
YOU WILL ONLY INAUGURATE YOUR STATUE YOURSELF, CHACHAJI.
THANKS, MADAM KUSAAD.
WOW ! IT RESEMBLES ME.
I SHOULD TAKE AT LEAST ONE SELFIE.

THIS STATUE WILL REMIND PEOPLE ABOUT YOU FOR A LONG TIME.
THAT'S TRUE.
I'LL LEAVE.
THANKS FOR COMING HERE CHACHAJI.
AFTER SOME DAYS.
MADAM KUSAAD, YOU HERE ? YOU SEEM TO BE VERY SCARED.

PRECIOUS STATUES ARE BEING STOLEN FROM OUR MUSEUM.
MANY STATUES HAVE BEEN STOLEN.
WE'RE UNABLE TO FIND THE THIEF OF THE STATUES.
IT'S A SERIOUS MATTER.
SOMETHING SHOULD BE DONE.
THIS WILL DO. *
* CHACHA CHAUDHARY'S BRAIN WORKS FASTER THAN A COMPUTER.

YOU BE ASSURED, MADAM KUSAAD, EVERYTHING WILL BE OK.
THANKS, CHACHAJI!
MUSEUM
SAME NIGHT.
BOSS HAS OPENED THE AUTOMATIC LOCK OF THE MUSEUM. LET'S GO INSIDE.
COME.
LIFT THE STATUES.

STOP.
TAKE ME ALONG WITH YOU.
WHO SPOKE ?
I.
OH ! THIS STATUE CAN SPEAK.
I DON'T JUST SPEAK...

I CAN JUMP ALSO...
... AND BEAT ALSO.
THUD!!
WHAMMM!
BANG!
AHHH!
THUD!

I HOPE YOU'VE COME TO KNOW BY NOW THAT I AM NOT A STATUE BUT CHACHA CHAUDHARY MYSELF.
WOW ! CHACHAJI. YOU'VE TACKLED THEM SINGLE HANDED.
HERE'S THE BOSS OF STATUE THIEVES, MADAM KUSAAD.
YOUR MANAGER GUTIYA.
HE KNEW THE VALUE OF YOUR STATUES.
THANKS CHACHAJI, YOU SAVED MY MUSEUM FROM GETTING RUINED.

CHACHA CHAUDHARY
AND
LAXMAN JHOOLA
ARE ALL THE ARRANGEMENTS DONE, DEAR.
YES.
JUST HAVE TO MAKE 40 CHAPATIS FOR SABU.
IT'S NOT REQUIRED. I'M NOT GOING TO RISHIKESH WITH YOU.

I'LL STAY AT HOME AND REST.
LET'S GO.
BYE !
CHACHA CHAUDHARY IS LEAVING WITHOUT SABU.
IT'S GOLDEN CHANCE TO FINISH HIM.
COME, LET'S FOLLOW HIM.

THE BUS REACHES RISHIKESH BUS STAND.
WE'LL GO STRAIGHT TO LAXMAN JHOOLA FROM HERE.
LAXMAN JHOOLA !!
WE'LL MAKE IT THE DEATH SWING FOR CHACHA CHAUDHARY.

WOW ! WHAT A BEAUTIFUL SCENE !
IT'S THE RIGHT TIME...
TO BLAST THE STEEL WIRE OF LAXMAN JHOOLA.
STEEL WIRE HAS BROKEN.
NOW CHACHA CHAUDHARY WON'T BE SPARED.

OH!
IT'S BREAKING!
WE'RE FALLING.
HA! HA! HA! NOW CHACHA CHAUDHARY'S FINISHED.
HA! HA! HA!

THEN-
NOTHING WILL HAPPEN TO CHACHAJI.
WHILE SABU IS THERE.
SABU ! YOU HERE ?
I'LL TELL YOU. FIRST YOU AND CHACHI GET DOWN.
COME MY DEAR.
SABU HAS SAVED HIM !

WHERE WILL YOU ESCAPE ?
GO TO JAIL.
OUCH ! OUCH !
I WAS FEELING LONELY WITHOUT YOU AT HOME, SO I FOLLOWED YOU AND CAME HERE.
THOUGH YOU WERE LATE, SABU, BUT STILL YOU REACHED ON TIME.

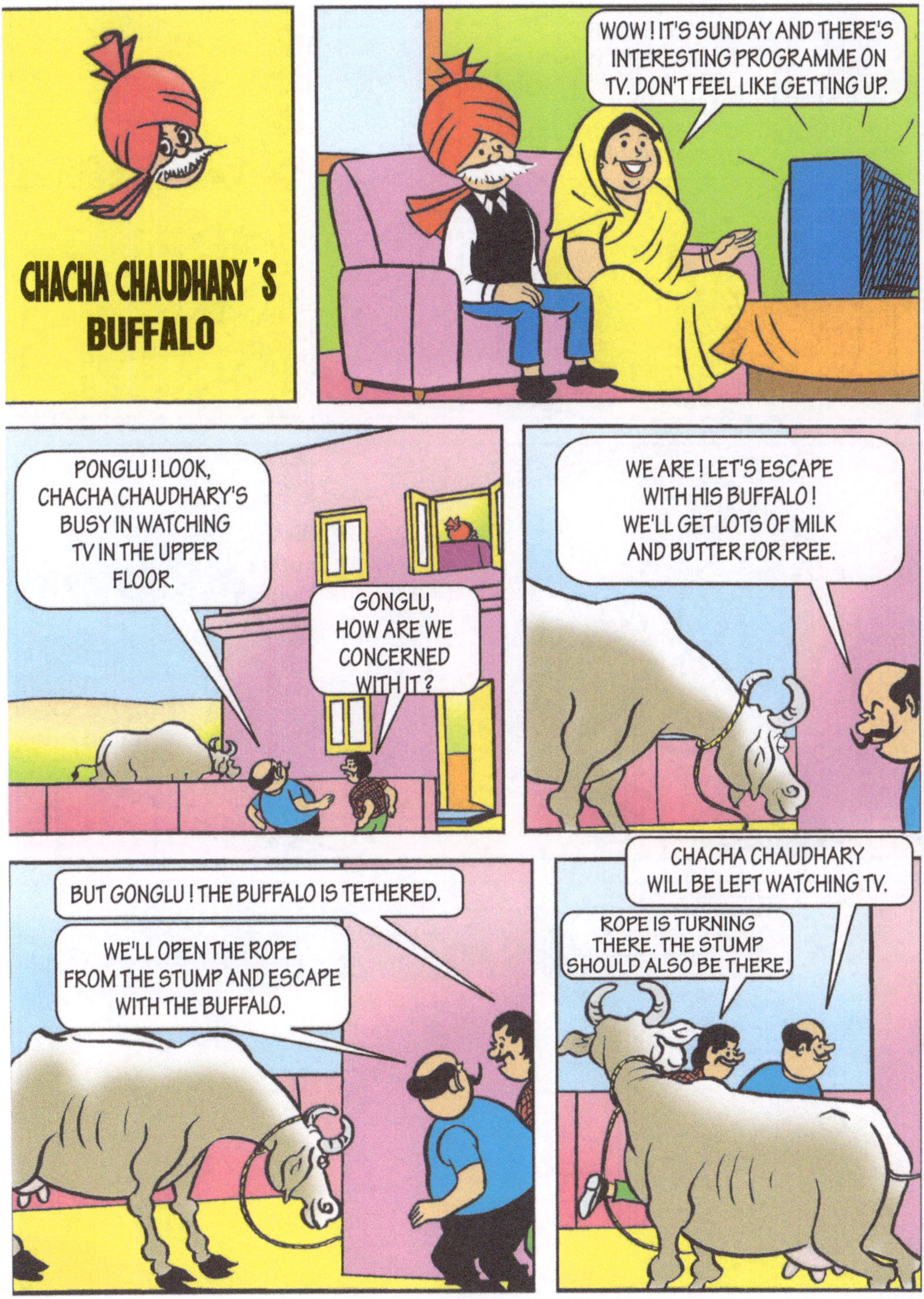
CHACHA CHAUDHARY 'S BUFFALO
WOW ! IT'S SUNDAY AND THERE'S INTERESTING PROGRAMME ON TV. DON'T FEEL LIKE GETTING UP.
PONGLU ! LOOK, CHACHA CHAUDHARY'S BUSY IN WATCHING TV IN THE UPPER FLOOR.
GONGLU, HOW ARE WE CONCERNED WITH IT ?
WE ARE ! LET'S ESCAPE WITH HIS BUFFALO ! WE'LL GET LOTS OF MILK AND BUTTER FOR FREE.
BUT GONGLU ! THE BUFFALO IS TETHERED.
WE'LL OPEN THE ROPE FROM THE STUMP AND ESCAPE WITH THE BUFFALO.
CHACHA CHAUDHARY WILL BE LEFT WATCHING TV.
ROPE IS TURNING THERE. THE STUMP SHOULD ALSO BE THERE.

ROPE IS STILL GOING FURTHER.
MAYBE THE STUMP IS AT THE BACK OF THE HOUSE. GOD KNOWS WHY CHACHA CHAUDHARY TIES SUCH A LONG ROPE TO THE BUFFALO.
ROPE IS GOING EVEN FURTHER.
BUT NOW IT'S ABOUT TO FINISH.
OH GOD !!
HA ! HA !!

CHACHA CHAUDHARY
AND
CONSTABLE DANDADIN
BUS STOP

BUS IS APPROACHING.

THERE WON'T BE ENOUGH SPACE FOR ME. I'LL TAKE THE NEXT BUS.

OH ! SOMEONE HAS PICKED MY POCKET. IT CONTAINED RS. 5000 .
WHY'RE YOU SHOUTING ? THIS IS CONSTABLE DANDADIN'S AREA. IT'S A CRIME AREA.
I KNOW WHO THE CULPRIT IS. KHACHCHU PICKPOCKET !
NO ! I HAVEN'T DONE ANYTHING.
ALL THIEVES SAY THIS.
YOU'VE BEEN IMPRISONED FOR 25 TIMES.
THIS TIME ALSO IT MUST BE YOU.
NOW I'VE LEFT ALL THIS.

CAN A SCORPIAN EVER CHANGE ITS NATURE ?
DANDADIN ! HE'S SAYING THAT CRIME IS NO LONGER HIS PROFESSION.
CHACHA CHAUDHARY ! SINCE WHEN HAVE YOU STARTED SHELTERING THIEVES AND GOONS ?
& CO
CONSTABLE ! AREN'T YOU AWARE OF VALMIKI ? HE WAS A DANGEROUS DACOIT...
AFTER HIS ATONEMENT, NOT ONLY DID HE BECOME A SEER, BUT ALSO WROTE THE MASTERPIECE RAMAYANA !
KHACHCHU ! SHOW YOUR POCKETS TO THE POLICEMAN.
LOOK ! THEY'RE EMPTY.
SO WHERE'S THE STOLEN MONEY ?
NAB THE ACTUAL CULPRIT BEFORE ESCAPING.

BUS STOP
SHE'S THE THIEF.
WHAT NONSENSE IS THIS ?
CHAUDHARY ! ARE YOU OUT OF YOUR MIND ? BOTH HER HANDS ARE TIED IN BANDAGE.
HOW CAN SHE DO IT?
SHE IS A CHEAT.
PLEASE FORGIVE ME. HERE'S THE RS. 5000 THAT I STOLE FROM THAT MAN.
MY MONEY.

CHACHA CHAUDHARY
AND FOUNTAIN
HANDLE
MY BALL !
SWISH !!
HIT !!
CRACK K !
GO AWAY ! PLAY
IN THE GROUND.

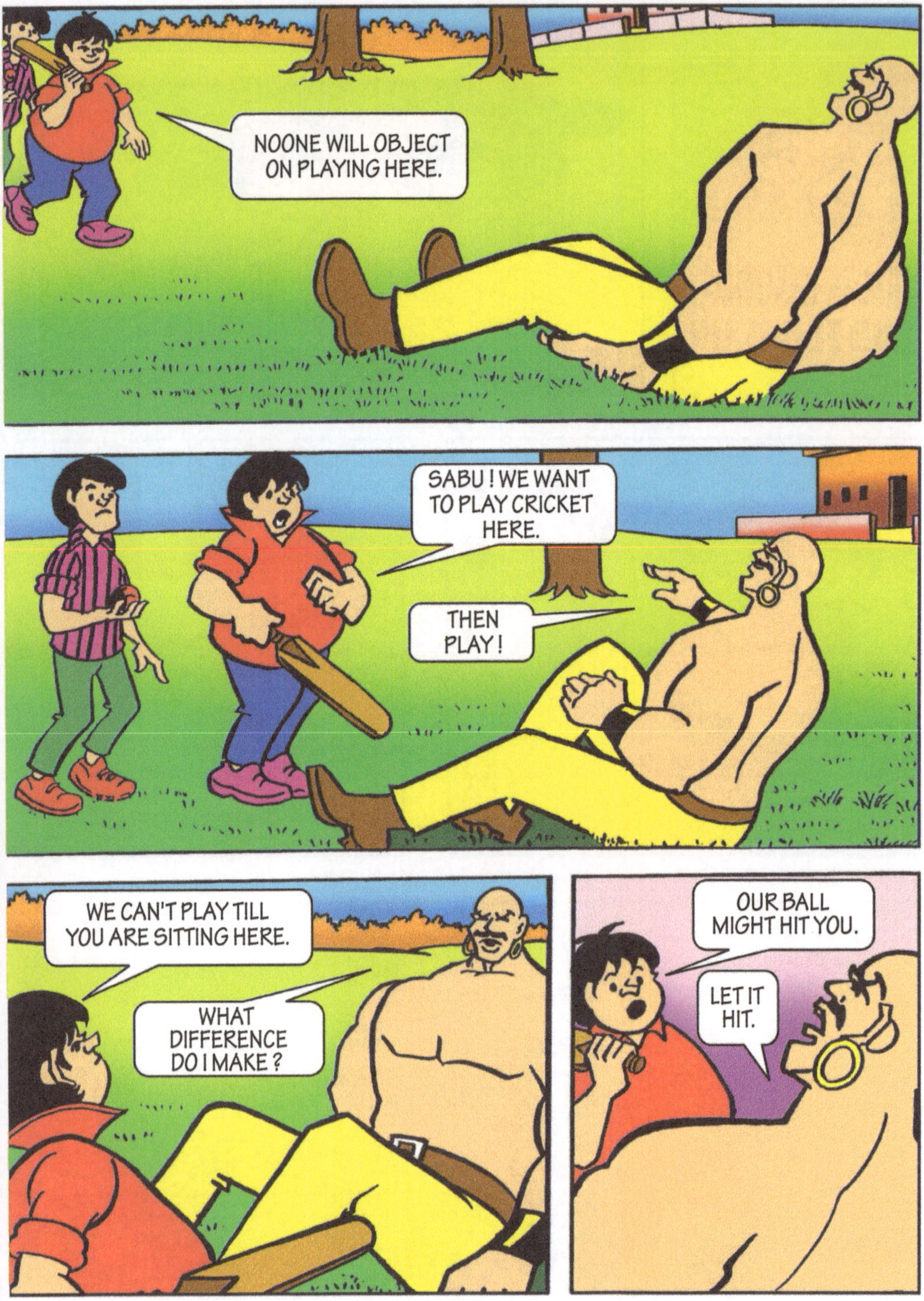
NOONE WILL OBJECT ON PLAYING HERE.
SABU ! WE WANT TO PLAY CRICKET HERE.
THEN PLAY !
WE CAN'T PLAY TILL YOU ARE SITTING HERE.
WHAT DIFFERENCE DO I MAKE ?
OUR BALL MIGHT HIT YOU.
LET IT HIT.

THE MOMENT IT HITS YOU, THE BALL WILL BREAK.
IF I GET UP, YOU WON'T BE ABLE TO PLAY.
GO FROM HERE. ONLY THEN WE'LL BE ABLE TO PLAY.
OK, I'LL GO.
I WAS SITTING ON THE FOUNTAIN.

CHACHA CHAUDHARY
EARRING AND WHEEL
CHACHAJI ! YOU HAD PROMISED THAT YOU WILL GIVE ME A TOY TO PLAY.
I SAID SO, RICKY ! BUT I DON'T HAVE MONEY FOR IT RIGHT NOW.
SO YOU GIVE ME SABU'S EARRING. I'LL USE IT AS A WHEEL.
YOU CAN HAVE IT, RICKY ! RETURN IT AFTER PLAYING.

WOW ! IT RUNS PERFECTLY.
THERE'S A SLOPE.
OH ! IT'S RUNNING AHEAD ! I CAN'T MATCH PACE WITH IT.
IRSHAH ! SOMEONE'S WHEEL HAS COME RUNNING TO US.
IT'S OF PURE GOLD ! IT'S WORTH THOUSANDS OF RUPEES.

MY WHEEL !
SHUT UP ! IF YOU MAKE NOISE, I'LL SLAP YOU.
BUDDAN ! USE YOUR BRAIN. IF HE CRIES, THERE'LL BE PROBLEM. THE POLICE MAY COME. LET ME HANDLE HIM.
MY GOOD BOY ! I'LL REPLACE YOUR SMALL WHEEL WITH THIS CYCLE'S WHEEL. IT'LL RUN FASTER.
OK ! RUN AWAY NOW !

RICKY! WHERE'S MY EARRING?
TWO ROGUES OVER THERE HAVE TAKEN IT...
AND GIVEN ME A CYCLE'S TYRE.
I DON'T TAKE OTHERS' BELONGINGS. WILL HAVE TO RETURN IT. COME WITH ME.
THEY'RE RUNNING AWAY.
GO!
SWISHHH !!

OUCHHH ! MY NECK !
THAT GOLD HAS FALLEN.
I'LL PICK IT UP !
?!
RUN !
WE LOST OUR CYCLE'S TYRE ALSO.

Word Puzzle

S	S	H	A	S	H	C	R	A	B
T	I	S	R	K	E	L	L	N	A
G	N	E	A	H	O	D	O	C	E
R	A	Y	L	O	R	O	L	P	H
S	Q	U	S	B	S	H	W	H	I
T	D	I	T	O	E	S	L	A	N
U	R	T	E	C	F	I	E	L	R
J	E	L	R	T	O	P	U	A	E
E	S	E	A	B	E	D	S	R	E
L	L	Y	F	I	S	H	C	O	F

ANEMONE
COD
CORAL REEF
CRAB
DOLPHIN
FISH
FLYING FISH
HALIBUT
HERRING
JELLYFISH
LOBSTER
MORAY EEL
MUSSEL
OCEAN
OCTOPUS

OYSTER
PLANKTON
SALMON
SCUBA DIVING
SEABED
SEAHORSE
SEAWEED
SHARK
SHELL
SQUID
STARFISH
STINGRAY
TURTLE
URCHIN
WHALE

S	A	L	M	A	N	E	M	E	T
S	M	O	O	P	N	K	O	N	U
T	A	R	N	L	A	T	O	N	B
S	R	A	Y	U	R	M	L	E	I
C	F	I	E	E	C	U	S	S	L
U	B	S	H	L	H	I	N	H	A
C	A	D	I	V	O	T	E	R	D
O	D	G	N	I	Y	S	G	S	E
F	I	N	H	S	E	H	N	E	E
L	Y	G	F	I	R	R	I	A	W

Complete this puzzle and send us back to win a surprise prize - write down the following details in block letter: Complete Name, Telephone Number with STD code (Mobile Number), Age, Place of Birth, Date of Birth, Gender, Email ID and Complete Postal Address with Pincode.